The Amazing Adventures of ABIOLA

Jeffrey & Debra Dean
Illustrated by Dwayne Ferguson

Africa World Press, Inc.

P.O. Box 1892
Trenton, New Jersey 08607

Africa World Press, Inc.
P.O. Box 1892
Trenton NJ 08607

Book Production coordinated at Africa World Press, Inc. by Carles J. Juzang

First Printing, 1994

Library of Congress Cataloging - in - Publication Data

Dean, Jeffery A., 1960-
    The amazing adventures of Abiola / by Jeffrey J. and Debra A. Dean ;
illustrations by Dwayne J. Ferguson.
        p. cm.
    Summary: An African American boy learns about his African heritage
and the accomplishments of other African Americans and is eager to
share this information with his friends at school.
    ISBN 0-86543-409-3 (hardback). -- ISBN 0-86543-410-7 (pbk.)
    [1. Afro-Americans--Fiction.   2. Afro-Americans--History-
-Fiction.] I. Dean, Debra A., 1963- . II. Ferguson, Dwayne J.
(Dwayne Joseph), ill. III. Title.
PZ7.D3442Am 1993
[Fic] -- dc20   93-30332
                                                          CIP
                                                           AC

Abiola is a very smart young African American boy. He enjoys learning about great African and African American accomplishments from his parents.

He enjoys learning
about great Africans

and African Americans

in many different fields
and sharing what he
learns with others.

Abiola goes to Sunshine
Elementary School. Today
is Abiola's first day in
a public school.

Abiola listens to his teachers. They talk about great men and women in history. Abiola looks at these men and women and realizes none of them are African or African American people.

During the next couple of months, Abiola is given very little information about African and African Americans' contributions to the world.

Abiola decided to talk to his teacher about this. His teacher, Mr. Finch said, "I understand your concerns and I'm sure we can work together to solve them. We like input from our students."

Abiola thought to himself,
my people as well as children
of other races and cultures
are being deprived of information
concerning African people's
contributions to the world.

This thought made Abiola sad.

Abiola decided to talk to his parents
about the problem he had in school.

Abiola's parents graduated from an historically black university, Alabama A & M University in Normal, Alabama. They were taught great facts about African and African American people. They always shared this information with Abiola.

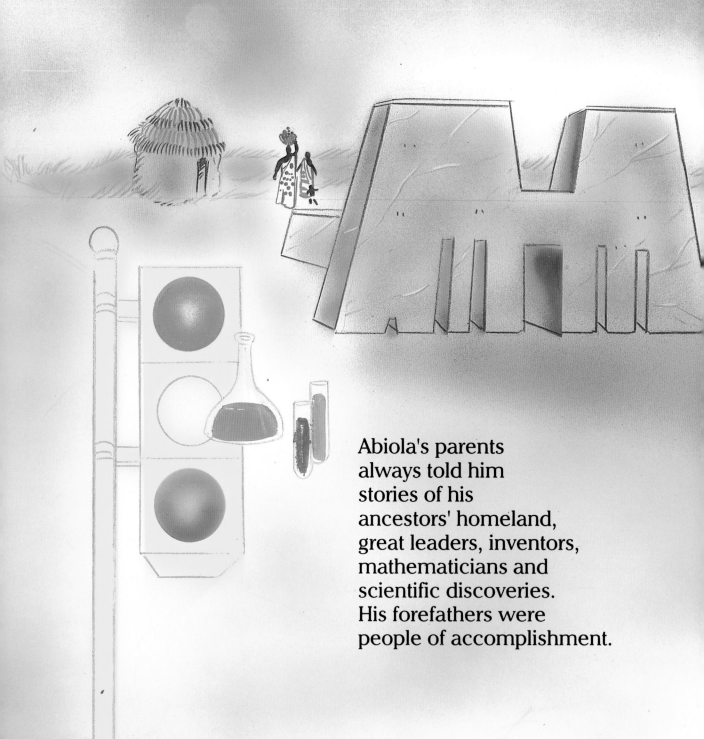

Abiola's parents
always told him
stories of his
ancestors' homeland,
great leaders, inventors,
mathematicians and
scientific discoveries.
His forefathers were
people of accomplishment.

Abiola's mother said, "Africa is where Africans and African Americans came from. Africa is a continent."

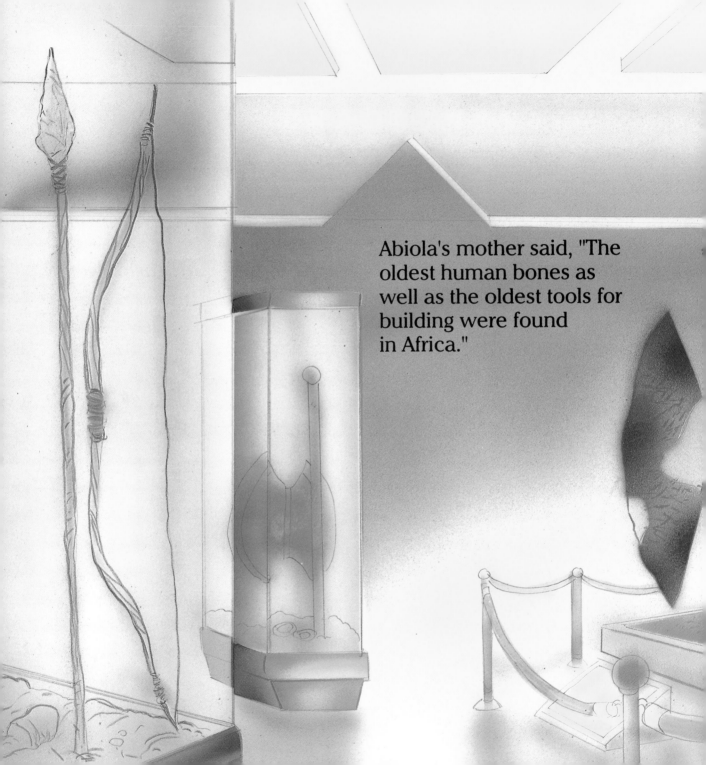

Abiola's mother said, "The oldest human bones as well as the oldest tools for building were found in Africa."

Abiola's father told him,
"Our people have accomplished
great feats for thousands of years."

Abiola's father said, "Just think about the pyramids and sphinxes which have been standing for thousands of years.

"Our people must have been tool builders as well as users, and must have had a great knowledge of math and science."

Abiola's father said,
"Africa is very rich
in natural resources,
which allowed great
African kings and
queens to trade with
the continent of Asia
as well as other
continents."

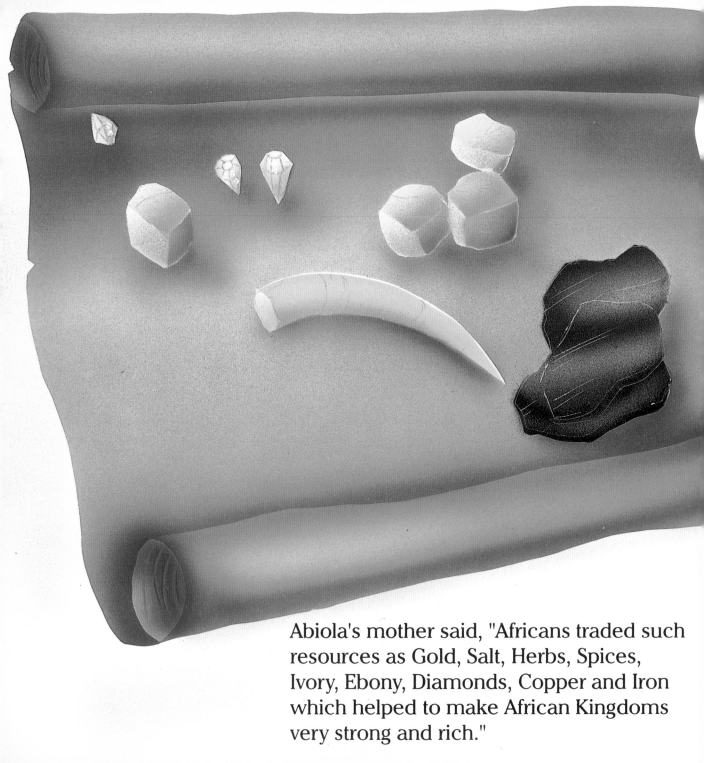

Abiola's mother said, "Africans traded such resources as Gold, Salt, Herbs, Spices, Ivory, Ebony, Diamonds, Copper and Iron which helped to make African Kingdoms very strong and rich."

Abiola remembered how excited he
became when his parents told him of
some of the great things his forefathers
accomplished.

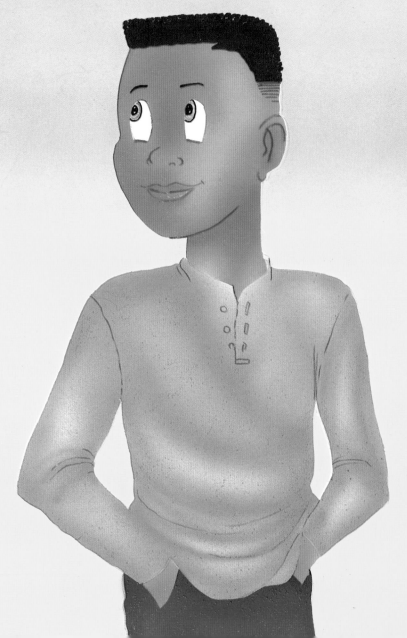

Abiola was so excited about what he had learned that he told all his friends what his father and mother taught him about Africa and African People.

Abiola's parents told him that there were many ways to gather information about his people's history and contributions, such as libraries and cultural festivals. Abiola's parents went on to give him examples of great African and African American men and women such as:

Dr. Charles Drew, who was a pioneer in blood preservation, as well as the founder of what we know today as blood banks.

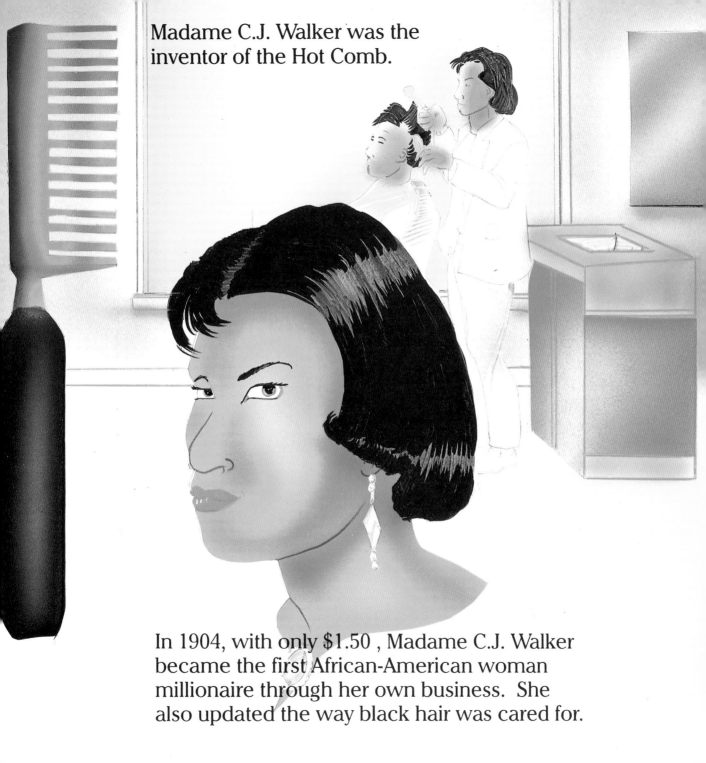

Madame C.J. Walker was the inventor of the Hot Comb.

In 1904, with only $1.50 , Madame C.J. Walker became the first African-American woman millionaire through her own business. She also updated the way black hair was cared for.

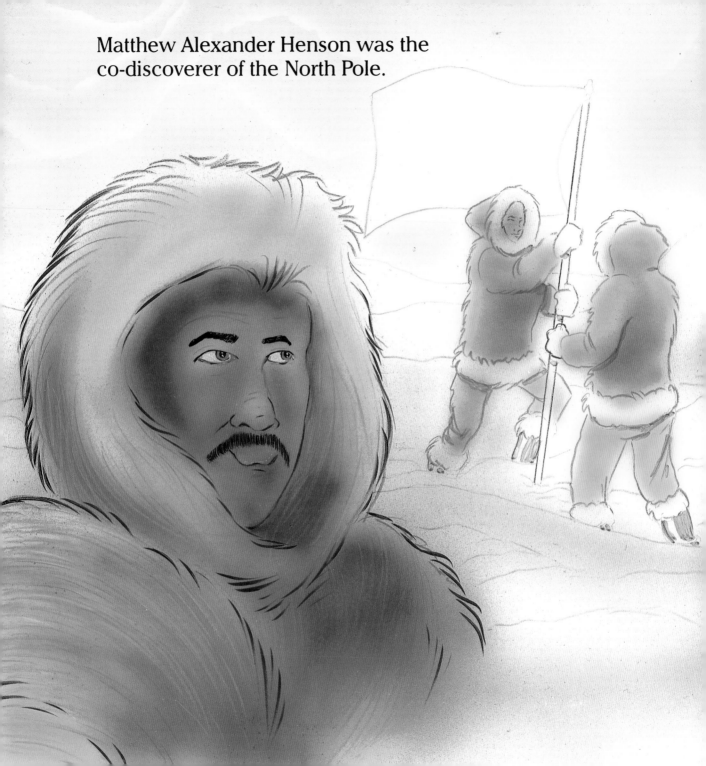

Matthew Alexander Henson was the co-discoverer of the North Pole.

Jean Baptiste Point Dusable discovered
and was the first settler of Chicago.

Barney Ford was a wealthy businessman, political activist and one of the early settlers of the state of Colorado.

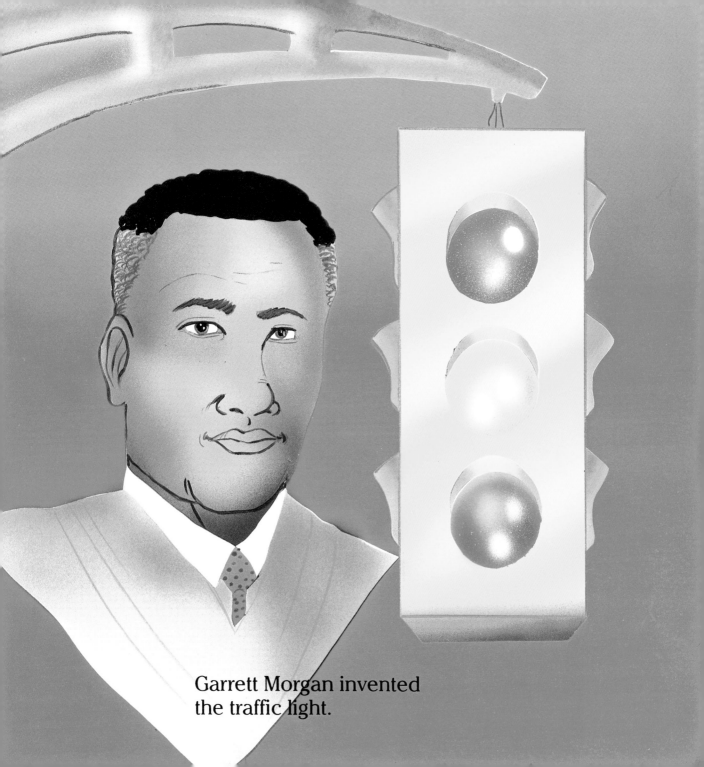

Garrett Morgan invented
the traffic light.

Katherine Johnson is an expert in the field of tracking and mapping for NASA.

Benjamin Banneker was responsible
for the design of Washington, D.C.

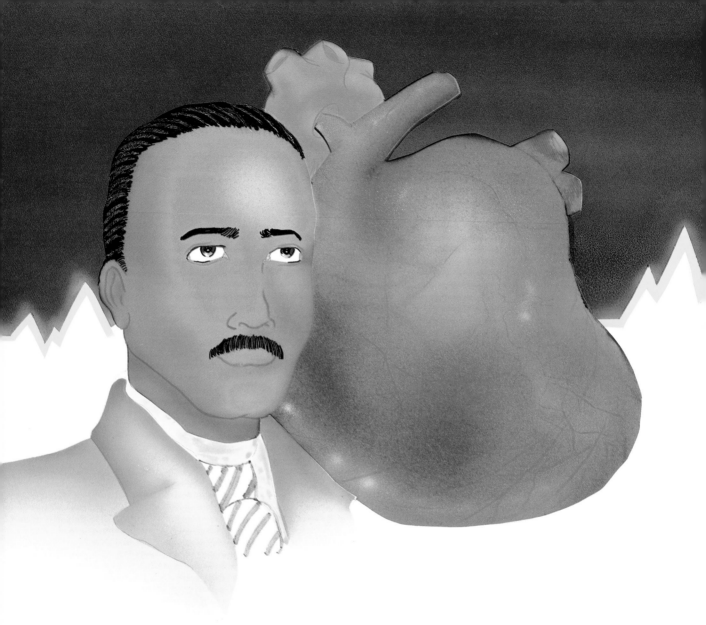

Dr. Daniel Hale Williams performed
the first successful open heart surgery.

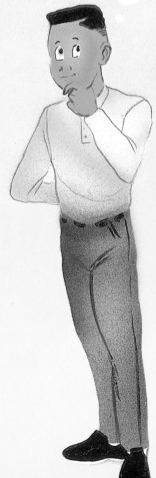

Abiola thought about all
the ways his parents said
he could gather facts about
his people.

He began to smile when he thought about
the adventures he would have while
searching for facts and sharing them with
other people.

This is surely not the end,
but only the beginning of:

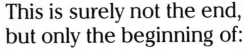

The Amazing Adventures of ABIOLA

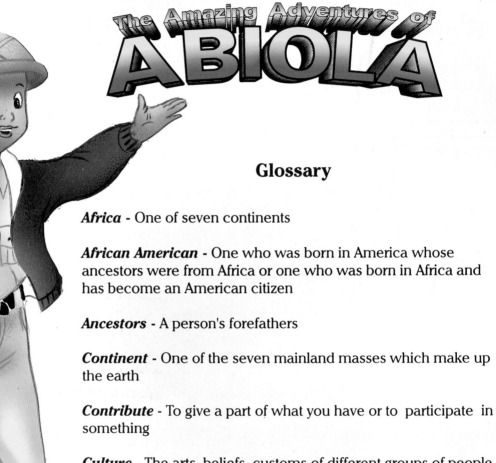

Glossary

Africa - One of seven continents

African American - One who was born in America whose ancestors were from Africa or one who was born in Africa and has become an American citizen

Ancestors - A person's forefathers

Continent - One of the seven mainland masses which make up the earth

Contribute - To give a part of what you have or to participate in something

Culture - The arts, beliefs, customs of different groups of people

Deprive - To take something away from

Invention - A new device, method or process developed from study or experiment

Pioneer - One who goes into unknown territory to settle